TIME I$ M🕐NEY

TIME I$ M●NEY

BRADY KUNZ &
THOMAS SUSSMAN

iUniverse, Inc.
Bloomington

Time I$ Money

iUniverse books may be ordered through booksellers or by contacting:

iUniverse
1663 Liberty Drive
Bloomington, IN 47403
www.iuniverse.com
1-800-Authors (1-800-288-4677)

ISBN: 978-1-4759-0599-1 (sc)
ISBN: 978-1-4759-0600-4 (e)

Printed in the United States of America

iUniverse rev. date: 03/27/2012

CHAPTER 1

It was a cold day in southern Illinois. Peter Thompson was riding home on his rusty, old bike he had found in the junkyard. Peter is a tall, skinny 15-year-old boy. He has brown, short hair and big brown eyes. He is handsome, but very shy and not much of an outgoing person. Peter comes from a poor family. It seems like they always have just enough to get by on the bills each month. He enjoys visiting the junkyard often looking for unique objects to collect and use.

Peter's favorite thing to collect is old newspapers. He enjoys reading about the past events that happened in the town of Trenton where he lives. The newspapers he likes to collect are right from his town. The paper is called "The Trenton Sun".

Trenton is a fairly large town. It has a huge mall with a variety of shops and restaurants that attract many people. The streets are always congested with traffic because people enjoy shopping at the unique stores and eating at the many enticing restaurants.

Peter's newspaper collection includes newspapers from the

20th century. His favorite newspaper to read was printed 23 years ago, back in 2012, when Trenton High School won the State Championship in basketball. His dad, Brady, was a player on that team. Peter grew up hearing stories about his dad's championship season.

Unfortunately, Peter and his dad didn't get along. In fact, they were exact opposites. Brady was a star athlete, played in a band, and had a lot of friends in high school. Peter, on the other hand, isn't a huge sports or music fan and only hangs out with Tyler, the boy in his class that lives in the apartment next door.

Peter wishes he and his dad were closer, but they have such different interests that it's hard for them to connect. When his dad wants to go shoot hoops, Peter would rather read his newspapers or go to the junkyard.

Peter had heard many of his dad's crazy stories from high school and wishes he was more of a livewire. The craziest thing he's ever done was sneak out with Tyler and go to the junkyard really late at night. He loved sitting on an old, worn-out, thrown-away recliner that sat precariously atop a big junk pile. There he would look up into the night's sky and stare longingly at the stars.

Peter always hated when people made fun of the junkyard or mistook it for a landfill. Landfills contain trash and old food for decomposition; it is the gross kind of trash. A junkyard is filled with old stuff. Sure you find some weird gross things there, but it's not like Peter would mull around on rotten food. Peter always told people the famous American proverb, "One man's trash is another man's treasure."

One amazing aspect about Trenton was that no matter where you were in town, you could always see the Big Dipper in the night sky. Peter's mother, Anna, always told him how amazing the Big Dipper looked back when she was a kid, and for some reason she says it's not quite the same anymore. She said it was probably the fact that Trenton is a lot bigger now, which means there are more lights reflecting on the sky. This makes it harder to see stars.

Peter and his mom were close. They did things together that Peter enjoyed, and she was supportive of Peter no matter what he did.

Peter's dad was the opposite. Brady wished Peter would be more like him. Unlike most kids, his dad played three sports in high school and was the best at each one. His dad was a star receiver for the football team in the fall, the center on the basketball team in the winter, and batted fourth in the line up for baseball in the spring.

Everyone thought Brady would get a scholarship to play one of these three sports in college, but when a tragic illness struck his parents, both receiving different types of cancer, he had to skip college and go to work to pay their medical bills.

Brady never had another opportunity to go to college, and now he works at a low paying job at the gas station.

Anna works part-time at the Trenton Sun, the local newspaper in Trenton. Peter is excited when his mom is able to bring him a newspaper every now-and-then fresh off the presses for him to add to his collection. A rush of excitement comes over Peter when he gets a newspaper a day before it is released. It's kind of like he is getting special treatment. It frustrates Brady because he would rather Peter be working out or playing some sort of sport instead of being cooped up in his room all day.

Peter finally arrived back at his apartment excited to look at the new newspaper he had found. It had all kinds of interesting stories from the past about the war in Iraq that happened many years ago. He was a history junky, which is why it was his favorite subject in school. Peter struggled in school and had to work tirelessly for his grades. Compared to his father and mother, his academic accomplishments were lacking, but he always was top in the class when it came to history.

Peter was so engrossed in the article he was reading that he didn't hear Tyler knocking on his door. Tyler was his best friend since preschool; they always had so much in common. Tyler was a short, skinny kid with fire-red hair. Tyler's family didn't have much more money than Peter's family did.

Tyler ran in the house because he was anxious to see if Peter wanted to go to the junkyard. Tyler didn't realize that Peter had just come from there. Peter showed him his newspaper. Tyler thought it was ridiculous that Peter collected newspapers, but Peter didn't care. He enjoyed reading about what was going on in the world and thought maybe the newspapers would be worth something someday.

Instead of going to the junkyard, they went straight to Peter's room, and turned on his PlayStation 3. Peter found the PS3 in the junkyard just two months ago; the PS3 is an old video game system that was popular around 2006 to 2013. Although the PlayStation 5 had been out for 2 years, Tyler and Peter always had a good time playing PS3.

The PS3 needed some repairs, but Peter fixed it up without a problem. Peter was good at fixing things for as long as he could remember. When he was little he used to take apart his toys and put them back together. Peter could take apart and put together any Game Boy in seconds. So when Peter found the PS3, it was easy to make it work like it did back in the day.

Peter even managed to save some money to obtain several used games for his PS3 from the gaming store in town.

Tyler and Peter's favorite game to play was FIFA 2012, which is a soccer game. Next to handiwork, Peter's best skill was playing video games. Whenever he would play FIFA, Peter would annihilate his opponents, which is what he did to Tyler.

Peter was winning 14-0 when Tyler's mom called and said he needed to go home. Tyler was a momma's-boy, so he obeyed immediately.

After Tyler left, Peter went back up to his room to read his new newspaper again. When he was finished, he filed the newspaper in his neatly organized collection. Peter had school the next morning and needed a good start to a boring Monday morning. He quickly showered and then headed to bed.

The next morning Peter woke up before his alarm. He laid in bed thinking for a while which he often did when he woke up early. He would think about the upcoming day, or the previous night. Random thoughts would run through his head. On this particular morning he thought about his father. It seemed like he thought about his father a lot. His dad was so cool, fun, and popular in high school. However, Peter felt like a loser; a loser who liked reading old newspapers, playing videogames, and spending his free time in a junkyard.

Peter has always wanted to be like his dad, but couldn't bring himself to do it. Peter tried sports, but that didn't work out. Peter tried music, but he couldn't develop a sense of rhythm. Peter tried to be more social and make friends, but it seemed like the only person who understands him is Tyler.

Peter and his dad's differences were not just one-sided. Peter's dad tried to participate in activities that Peter liked.

He would attempt to read newspapers with him, but they always ended up arguing about Peter's lack of exercise or something pointless. Peter and his dad are not meant to be similar.

CHAPTER 2

BEEP! BEEP! BEEP! With one roll, Peter got out of bed and off to start his day. He met Tyler at the bus stop, and they waited for its arrival.

"I'm not looking forward to school today. Mondays are always boring," said Tyler.

"Tell me about it," agreed Peter. "The only highlight of my day is going to be the chicken nuggets we get to eat for lunch, even though they have no taste."

Peter and Tyler hopped on the bus and sat in their usual seats in the front. They wanted to sit in the back, but that's where the "cool" kids sat.

One day the bus driver went to Peter and Tyler's stop first, so they were the first ones on the bus. They tried to run back to the back and take a seat in the very last row. Unfortunately, at the next stop, one of the cooler kids strolled down the aisle and asked what they were doing and made fun of them, until they embarrassingly walked back to the front of the bus.

Peter and Tyler just weren't accepted by the other kids.

The most popular kids were the good-looking athletes that had a little group that ran the school. Peter wanted to hang with those kids, but he knew they wouldn't let him unless he was more like his dad.

Frankly, nobody liked who Peter was, not even Peter. He would give anything to be like his dad. His mom and Tyler were the only people who accepted him for the way he is. Together, Peter and Tyler walked into the school waiting to start their boring Monday.

Every morning Peter and Tyler go to the cafeteria and sit at their usual table in the corner and talk. Nobody comes to talk to them or acknowledge that they even exist, but they don't mind. They enjoy the privacy.

Today they were talking about girls. But not just girls in general, they were talking about the two prettiest girls in the school, Sarah Welch and Leslie Campbell. Sarah and Leslie were sophomores, too. Sarah was a blonde, had the prettiest green eyes, she was tall, and very smart. Leslie was also tall, but unlike Sarah, she had red hair and was not very smart. Tyler had a crush on Leslie, and Peter had a crush on Sarah. Tyler and Peter knew that they had no chance, but being alone in the corner of the lunchroom, they could talk about these girls with no worries of anyone hearing. It was a coincidence then, when Sarah and Leslie both walked by. Peter noticed them in time to change the subject to the history test they were going to have today.

"Hey, Peter!" Sarah greeted, with a smile.

"Oh, hey…Sarah! What's up?" Peter replied, trying his best to smile, but he knew his face was as red as an apple.

No response. Sarah and Leslie just walked on by. *At least she said something to me,* Peter thought to himself.

Peter used to live next to Sarah when they were little. Back then she lived with her single mom and her name was Sarah Locksley. She lived in apartment A-8 and Peter lived in A-7. They used to play and have fun together. Peter has always had a crush on her, even when they were little. Then Sarah's mom married a man who was wealthy. They moved across town to the nicer neighborhood, called the North Land Acres. She made new friends and became extremely popular. Now she and Peter don't talk or hang out anymore because Sarah is busy with her other friends.

The morning bell rang. Peter and Tyler both got up to go to class.

Peter's first class of the day was history. He enjoys starting his day off with a class that he is extremely fascinated with. Tyler wasn't in first hour history, so Peter just talked to the teacher, Mr. Bell.

Mr. Bell was a hefty guy, it always seemed like he was bigger wide than he was tall. As soon as everyone arrived in the classroom, Mr. Bell handed out the test. Peter finished it in 10 minutes, first one done. With 40 minutes left of class, Peter sat around and read his book.

His next period was health with Mrs. Lane. Mrs. Lane was a short, elderly woman. Rumor says that she is pushing 90 years old. Today, in her classroom, they were watching a video on drugs which had to be a quarter of a century old. Peter just zoned out the whole time. Before he knew it, the class ended and he headed off to study hall.

The rest of his day went pretty good, but nothing special. Peter was just looking forward to heading home and going to the junkyard. He hoped to find anything new that would give him something to do. Finally, the day ended. The bus took Peter and Tyler to their stop, and they started walking home.

"You coming to the junkyard today, Tyler?" asked Peter.

"No, not today. I've got to finish my book report for English class," Tyler replied. "That class is so hard."

"Okay, well, I'll let you know if I find anything awesome," Peter said. "I feel like today's going to be a good day."

When they finally arrived home, Tyler headed inside to start his report. Peter walked into his apartment and saw his dad.

"Hey, Pete, want to go shoot around a little bit?" Peter heard his dad say.

His dad was spinning a basketball on one finger; he was dressed in athletic shorts and a t-shirt, ready for some exercise.

"Well…I was going to go to the junkyard to look for something cool," Peter replied hesitantly.

"Oh…" Brady said.

Peter could see the disappointment in his eyes.

"Well, I'll see you later, Dad," Peter said.

He put his schoolbag away and headed out the door. Peter couldn't help but to be sad. He wants so badly to be closer to his dad, but they are just too different. He hopes that something will be at the junkyard to cheer him up. Peter was so anxious to get to the junkyard that he pedaled his bike as quickly as possible and began to wander around.

CHAPTER 3

Peter loves the feeling he gets when he first walks into the junkyard, so many items and treasures to be found in it. He starts on the west side of the junkyard and has his head down looking to see what he can find. He finds an old, broken watch, a Rolex actually; he tinkers with it a little bit and finds that it cannot be fixed.

The next cool thing that Peter finds is an old Fender Telecaster guitar. *Dad would get a kick out of this,* he thought. He puts it back down and starts looking for something else.

Finally after an hour of looking, something finally catches his eye. It was a box, sealed up with tape. He could tell it hadn't been opened since it was sealed. Peter picked it up. It felt light, like it was just paper. Peter opened it up by tearing off the tape in one clean strip. He looked inside and was surprised to find an old lottery ticket. Peter thought that was pretty cool. He's found lottery tickets before. A couple months ago Peter won 10 dollars with a 1998 lottery ticket. It's not like Peter could cash these in. Some are so old, half of the lottery companies are gone. Peter wondered why someone would seal up a box with only one lottery ticket. Maybe, he thought, just maybe, it was a big winner. Peter decided to keep it.

After a long day of looking, all he had in his hands at the end was the ticket. He was not as enthusiastic riding home that evening. As soon as he arrived home, he went to his room to play video games. With just five minutes remaining in his game, his dad walked in.

"Hey, bud, whatcha find today?" his dad, Brady, asked him, trying to seem interested.

"Nothing really, just an old lottery ticket," Peter replied.

"From how long ago?" Brady asked.

"March of 2012," Peter said, while looking at the ticket.

"Oh, those were the days...I remember when...," Brady responded. But Peter zoned out and thought to himself, *Oh, here we go again, another story about my cool dad.*

"....and after I hit that shot, it was over, we won state. We were champs. I ended up with 41 points that game, too," Brady finished.

"Oh, that's awesome, Dad. I wish me and Tyler did things like you guys did when you were young."

Peter said that because he knew that's what his dad wanted to hear.

"You guys should try sometime. All it takes is a little practice," Brady suggested, before he walked out of Peter's room.

Peter actually did wish they would do things like that. Nevertheless, he felt like the junkyard was cool enough for them.

Peter stared at the lottery ticket. He decided to look at his newspaper collections to read his dad's State Championship article. He looked and saw papers from *March 2007, March*

2012, March 2008, ah, here we go Sunday, March 11ᵗʰ, 2012, he thought.

Peter looked at the front page like he has done hundreds of times before. He saw the famous championship picture on the front page with his dad and all of his friends standing proud, showing off their trophy.

Trenton High School State Champions starting five celebrate with their trophy, in order from left to right, Alex Moore, Mitch Williams, Brady Thompson, Thomas Jones, and Mike Johnson

Peter kept reading the article below the picture.

Trenton High School's basketball team won the state championship yesterday. The team traveled to Peoria, Illinois to compete. They barely won their Super-Sectional game by one point in overtime against Breese High School to send them to state.

In the state tournament, they were seeded last as the underdogs. In the first game, forward Thomas Jones put up 29 points, with 6 assists, and 3 rebounds to get the win against Chicago Public High School.

The next game, Alex Moore put up 8 points with 9 assists, Mitch Williams had 10 points and 12 rebounds, Thomas Jones had 14 points and 6 assists, Mike Johnson put up 22 with 11 assists, and Brady Thompson put up a whopping 41 points, 10 assists, and 15 rebounds. Brady also made the game winning shot for the huge win over Carbondale High School to win the state championship. Congratulations, Trenton Warriors.

Peter could almost recite that article perfectly without reading. He flipped to the next page, more State Champs stuff. He skimmed the article on the President of the United States.

Then he went to the back page, The Classifieds. *2003 Dodge Ram for sale, House for sale, Drum set for sale,* Peter read on, *Lotto winners*. Peter stopped reading. He pulled out the ticket he found earlier in the junkyard. It read *33-27-4-19-21-16*. The numbers matched perfectly with the numbers in the newspaper. *He was a winner! He had won 100 million dollars! Just my luck,* thought Peter, *if only it were 2012 again.*

If Peter had 100 million dollars it would change everything. His family would no longer be poor, and he could live in a beautiful house in a nice neighborhood with all the popular kids. He could live next to Sarah again. This unbelievable turn of events made Peter think about his life and how he wished things were different.

Peter decided to sneak to the junkyard that night and think about things while looking at the night sky. He found the tallest junk pile and perched himself on top. He looked at the stars and saw the Big Dipper. Then he saw something odd. A shooting star was passing right through the Big Dipper.

A shooting star, time to make a wish, Peter thought jokingly.

"I wish I could go back to 2012 and claim that money, which would fix everything," Peter whispered to himself before drifting off to sleep.

CHAPTER 4

Peter woke up on the ground. He was confused; he couldn't remember if he made it home last night or not. He saw a slide, a swing set, and a see-saw. Then he finally noticed the sign saying "Nut House Park." It was a beautiful spring day. Birds were chirping, the sky was blue, and it was about 65 degrees.

Where am I? He thought, *I've never been to this park and plus, it was like 20 degrees last night! How could the weather change so dramatically?*

Peter checked his watch. It was 9:00 in the morning, he was late for school! He leaped up off the ground and ran. He eventually found West Broadway Street, which is the main road in Trenton.

Peter was in such a hurry he did not notice that everything looked a little hazy, and by that, everything seemed a little different. Nevertheless, Peter thought it was because he just woke up.

He ran up Broadway and eventually arrived at Trenton

High School. He continued to hurry inside the backdoors and straight to his locker. Peter tried his combination three times before he started wondering if he was at the wrong locker.

Locker 365. Am I at the right locker? he thought.

Then Peter heard the bell. *Oh, first hour must be over. Dangit! I missed history…maybe I can just sneak into second hour and no one will notice I was gone first hour.*

This is when a tall, muscular, brown-haired boy approached him.

"Hey, dude, what are you doing at my locker?" the boy asked of Peter.

"Uh…this is my locker," a really confused Peter responded.

"It's my locker…watch…," the boy commanded, while pushing Peter out of the way.

He entered his combination and the locker opened on the first try. Then Peter peered inside.

Where are my books? These aren't mine, he thought.

Then Peter ran to Mrs. Lane's class. When he walked inside, he knew no one. At first he thought he'd walked into the wrong class, because all of the students weren't familiar. Even Mrs. Lane wasn't there. Instead, it was some middle-aged, blonde teacher.

"Excuse me! I think I'm in the wrong class," Peter said to the teacher.

"Oh, good heavens! It's March and you don't even know your way around the school? What class are you looking for?" she inquired of Peter.

"I'm looking for Mrs. Lane's health class," he answered, very confused.

"Well, you've come to the right place! I'm Mrs. Lane, you

can take a seat at the empty desk over there," she directed, pointing to the back corner.

Peter hesitantly walked to the back corner and took "his seat." The kid in front of Peter turned around.

"Oh, what's poppin', new kid?" the kid in front of Peter asked.

"I'm not a new kid. I'm really confused today and everything is different," Peter replied. "Who are you, anyways?"

"Me? I'm Thomas Jones, pretty much the coolest kid at THS," Thomas bragged to Peter.

Thomas was a shaggy, brown-haired kid. He looked athletic, too. He had blue eyes and very straight, white teeth. He was well-dressed, wearing jeans and a plaid button-up shirt. You could tell he was outgoing.

"Oh, well, it's nice to meet you. I'm Peter Thompson," Peter advised.

"Alright, Petey…it's a pleasure," Thomas said back.

Thomas turned around and health class started. Mrs. Lane said that we were watching a video about drugs today that came out 2 years ago. Five minutes into the video, Peter noticed that it was the exact same video Mrs. Lane played for them yesterday. Peter's head was spinning. He did not know what was happening.

CHAPTER 5

After a very confusing morning at school, Peter was ready for lunch. They all walked through the lunch line like a herd of cattle being put into a pen.

He thought to himself, *Chicken nuggets again, how many times will they serve them in a row before we catch on?*

He went to sit down in his usual spot. He sat down and spent about five minutes wondering why Tyler was not at school. Then, he ate by himself. When Peter was nearly done eating, he heard a familiar voice.

"Yo, Petey! Come sit with us, my man!"

It was Thomas Jones. Peter got up and sat down next to Thomas.

"Hey guys, this is my boy, Petey," Thomas said to his friends at the lunch table while slapping Peter on the back. "Pete, this is Mike, Mitch, and Alex," Thomas informed Peter.

Mike was a tall, muscular, light-brown haired, tan boy with a friendly face. Mitch was a lanky boy with hair that was so blonde it almost looked white. Alex was a shorter kid with light brown hair, sporting a blonde highlighted patch of hair on the top.

"Hey guys, I'm Peter," Peter said to everyone.

"What up, P-money?" said the guys.

"Who's this tool?" said a voice from behind Peter.

"Oh, this is our boy, Peter. He's a new kid," Thomas said.

Peter turned around to see the person behind him. It was a tall, tan, muscular boy with short, dark hair.

"Peter, this is Brady," Thomas quickly related.

"Nice to meet you," Peter responded.

By now Peter's head was about to explode.

What was going on, he wondered. *First some other kid has his locker, Mrs. Lane looked 20 years younger, and now he's eating lunch with boys he had never met before.*

"Yeah, yeah, yo G, let me see your Spanish homework real quick," said Brady.

Thomas pulled out his homework for Spanish class. Peter glanced at the date which read, *Monday, March 5th, 2012.* Then the events of his bewildering day started to make sense. He was in the past!

The boys he had just eaten lunch with were the same kids from the article that he had practically memorized about the 2012 State Championship. He just had been called a tool by his own father!

Peter didn't know what to think. His wish had come true and now he's stuck in 2012 with his father and his friends.

Peter started making conversation to assure himself that his idea of his being in the past was correct.

"Do you guys play basketball?" he asked.

"Yeah, we all do. We got the 1st round of the State Tournament on Wednesday," Alex replied excitedly.

Peter then remembered about the lottery ticket in his pocket.

Great, thought Peter, *I'm stuck here for another week until the lotto drawing.* Then more questions entered Peter's thoughts. *Where will I stay? How will I get home? What if they find out I'm from the future?*

"Oh, that's awesome! Good luck," Peter shouted his support.

"Thanks, Petey," said Alex. "So, where you from, new kid?" he inquired of Peter.

"Uh…up north," said Peter, trying to think of something to say.

"Oh, are you Canadian, eh?" asked Mitch.

"No, I'm from…Chicago," Peter replied, finally getting an idea to spring into his brain.

"Empire State Building…nice," said Alex.

"Alex, you say the most ridiculous things ever," Brady criticized.

"Yeah, can you believe this joker, Petey?" Mike asked.

"Yeah, he's a real…toolbox," Peter quickly thought of something to say.

"Ha, ha! Nice, Petey," laughed Michael.

"I like you already," Mitch agreed.

The group had a nice laugh and everyone started liking Peter, even Alex, although he was just insulted.

Unexpectedly, a girl walked by the table. She had long, brown hair, big, blue eyes, and an amazing smile. Peter couldn't help but to stare.

"Who's that?" Peter asked. "She's a babe!"

"Whoa! Back off, Jack! That's Anna and she's MY girl!" said Brady angrily.

"Oh," Peter said, he couldn't believe he had just called his mother a babe. "I'm sorry...I didn't know she was your girlfriend."

"She's not his girlfriend," informed Alex.

"Yeah, he's just had a crush on her since junior high," chimed in Michael.

"Shut up! Some day she will like me...I know it," optimistically spoke Brady.

Peter laughed.

"Hey! What's so funny?" Brady asked.

"Nothing," Peter said, still laughing. "I think she will like you, too."

"So you guys up for some Dairy King after school?" Mitch said, changing the subject.

"Sure thing, I'm in," Thomas replied, while Alex, Michael, and Brady agreed with him. "You up for it, Pete-Miester?"

Peter thought about it for a little.

"Sure! What's Dairy King?" Peter replied. "I've only heard of Dairy Queen."

Michael choked on his chocolate milk.

"You don't know what Dairy King is?" Michael exclaimed.

"Of course, he doesn't, Mike. All they know in Chicago is pizza and Derrick Rose," Thomas said to Mike.

"And the Empire State Building!" Alex said, trying to back up his last dumb statement.

"Who's Derrick Rose?" a confused Peter asked. "And will someone please tell me who The Dairy King is?"

"Derrick Rose is a superstar guard for the Chicago Bulls," said Thomas. "How can you not know that? And Dairy King is a little burger joint in Trenton. They have great food and Ski, which is a local soda around here. It's amazing!"

Peter obviously knew about Ski, but he had to keep his cover as a student from Chicago.

"Ski?" Peter repeated, pretending to be confused. "That sounds awesome. Yeah, I can go."

"Cool, I'll give you a ride there after school. Meet me in the parking lot," Thomas said, just as the bell rang, signifying the end of lunch.

While everyone got up to go to their next class, Peter's mind was about to explode.

This is crazy, he thought, *I just ate lunch with my dad and his friends he always talks about, and I'm going to hang out with them after school!*

CHAPTER 6

Peter was excited to see what his dad was like as a kid. He had heard stories, but now he will get to see for himself. Peter hoped that maybe in the past he could find some connection with his dad.

For the remaining portion of the school day, Peter just played off like being the new student from Chicago that he said he was. He had no classes for the rest of the day with his dad or his dad's friends. But when the final bell rang, Peter was eager to get out to the parking lot to meet Thomas.

As he was walking outside to the parking lot, he heard someone say, "Hey, Peter!"

It was a girl's voice, a very familiar voice to Peter.

Sarah? Peter thought.

He turned around. It wasn't Sarah but a girl who could have been her twin. She had long, blonde hair and beautiful green eyes just like Sarah.

"Um…hey," Peter said. "How do you know my name?"

"Well, I saw you talking with Brady and his friends, so I

asked him who you were. He told me you were Peter, the new kid from Chicago. I thought I would come welcome you to our school, although I'm a little late," she laughed and smiled, then said, "Well…see you tomorrow, Peter."

Peter noticed she had a gorgeous smile as she walked away. Peter didn't know what just happened, but all he knew was that she was extremely pretty. Peter realized then that he had a little crush on her.

Thomas then approached Peter.

"Petey, you ready to head to DK?" Thomas asked.

"Yeah. Who was that?" Peter asked him.

"That, my friend, is Taylor Locksley, one of the hottest girls in school," Thomas answered.

Locksley, hum…where had Peter heard that before? He then remembered that it was Sarah's mom's maiden name. Had he a crush on Sarah's mom?

"Oh!" Peter said, still thinking about what he had discovered. "She seems nice."

"Oh, she's nice alright," Thomas said in a joking manner. "Looks like somebody has a crush on her."

"No, I don't," Peter was smiling. He knew he had been caught.

"Don't worry, P-Dog. My girlfriend, Tiffany, is her best friend. I'll put in a good word for you."

They piled in the car and headed to Dairy King to meet with the gang. Thomas's car was nice. It was obviously somewhat new, a nice red color, and a smooth leather interior. As they were driving along, Peter turned on the stereo. "I'VE GOT ANOTHER CONFESSION TO MAKE!" he heard blare from the speakers.

"Whoa! What's this?" Peter asked.

"You never heard of Foo Fighters? It's Brady's favorite band. He must have left his CD in my car."

"No, I haven't," Peter said while wondering why his father had neglected to tell him about his favorite band.

We really aren't close at all, Peter thought.

"These guys are pretty good," Peter said.

"Yeah, man, I think they are solid, but Brady is obsessed. He once listened to one of their songs for four hours straight. What a freak, right?"

"Totally," Peter said. He couldn't believe his dad had such a passion for something and didn't share it with him.

"If it wasn't for them, Brady and I wouldn't be in a band," Thomas said.

"You two are in a band?" Peter asked, although he knew the answer.

"Yeah, we are called 'Up To Know Good'," Thomas replied.

Wow, Peter thought, *Dad never even told me the name of his band.* Peter was starting to get upset.

"That's awesome! What instruments do you guys play?" Peter asked.

"I'm on drums, while Brady sings and plays his guitar," Thomas explained.

"Sweet!" Peter did know that. His dad still played guitar from time to time.

"You should come to a gig sometime," Thomas invited.

"Sure," Peter said.

He would take any chance he could find, just to get closer to his dad.

They pulled into a building at the corner of a four way. Peter stepped out of the car and saw a green neon sign with a cartoon-like penguin on it: Dairy King. They were here. Peter then looked around. He noticed how different Trenton looked. It wasn't some busy town like the Trenton in his time. It was a small country town with a few gas stations, banks, restaurants, and stores.

"Do you guys have a mall here?" Peter asked Thomas.

"Nah, Trenton is just a little town with a few shops and places to eat," he replied. "There are more churches than banks."

Peter was amazed. He had no idea Trenton used to be a small town. He didn't even know there used to be a Dairy King. His dad never talked about what Trenton was like when he was young. Peter was surprised it didn't always have the mall. He just assumed it had always been here.

They walked into Dairy King and sat down with the gang.

"Hey, guys," Thomas greeted.

"I ordered you and Peter a burger and a Ski," Brady said.

"Thanks, dude," Thomas replied.

"You're in for a treat, man…this will change your life," Michael said, joining the conversation.

"I can't wait!" Peter exclaimed.

"So, Peter, what do you like to do?" Mitch asked him.

"I like to umm…play video games," Peter said, hoping they would think it was cool.

"Nice, you have a PS3? That's what I have at my house. You will have to come over and play with us sometime. We are kind of on a FIFA kick. I don't know if you've ever played it before," Brady said excitedly.

"Yeah, I love FIFA. I'm pretty good," Peter bragged.

"Oh, we will see about that! I've never lost before," Brady said confidently.

Peter was excited. He was bonding with his father. He knew it was a kid version, but he didn't care. He didn't realize his dad used to love to play video games especially FIFA. He wished he had invited his dad to play with him sometime, but he was afraid his dad would think it was lame. He knew the first thing he was going to do when he arrived back home.

Home, Peter thought, h*ow am I going to get back?*

Then he realized he didn't want to go back. He had friends here, and he was close to his dad. To top it all off, he was going to be 100 million dollars richer. Things just kept getting better and better for Peter.

"Hey, where do you go to cash in lottery tickets?" Peter asked, while pulling out the ticket.

"Let me see that," said Brady. "That looks like you got it from C.C. Food Mart, the gas station from down the street. Don't think you're going to win anyway...the lottery is impossible."

"I was just wondering. I'm feeling kind of lucky," Peter said.

"Whatever, dude! The drawing isn't until Saturday night, after the State Championship," Brady confirmed.

"Thanks, if I win I'll give you guys a cut," Peter promised.

"Sounds like a plan to me," said Brady, with everyone else agreeing.

They didn't realize that Peter's ticket would win. They were about to become State Champions and a whole lot richer on Saturday.

When the food and drinks arrived, they all ate, drank and talked.

"This is awesome...why did this place ever close down?" Peter asked before he could stop himself.

"What are you talking about? It's still here, you goon," Alex laughed at Peter, thinking he was very confused.

"Um...I meant does this place ever close? Because I'm feeling a late night run back up here," Peter recovered quickly.

"A late night run, that's my kind of guy," Michael said. "Hey, Brady, you think he should join in the nugget fest?"

"Nugget fest?" Peter asked.

"Yeah, on the night after we win the first round of state, we are celebrating by eating 150 nuggets...just the five of us. With six, we will go for...what do you think, Brady, 200?" Alex asked.

"That sounds good; you're in, new kid. You better bring your A-Game," Brady said.

"I will!" Peter answered.

They got up to leave.

"Brady, can you take Peter home? Tiffany texted me five times in the last hour to remind me I needed to help her "study" tonight," winked Thomas, while smiling on the word "study."

"Yeah, I guess," Brady agreed.

CHAPTER 7

They headed to Brady's car and hopped in. His car was nice, too. It was black exterior, with a sunroof, and it also had white, leather seats. This was the chance Peter had been waiting for; a chance to bond with his father without worrying about being like him or making him proud. By now, Peter saw Brady as his friend not his father. He felt like he could be himself around his dad for the first time in his life. Brady pulled out and they started to drive.

"So, you and Thomas are in a band together, right?" Peter asked.

"Yeah, we're playing a gig Friday night at Jane Brown's party. You gonna go to that?" Brady inquired.

"I wasn't invited. I have no clue who Jane Brown is," Peter responded.

"Oh, well, Jane and I are friends. I'll get you an invite."

"Thanks, man," Peter said.

"So you got your eyes on any girl yet?" Brady asked.

"Well, Taylor Locksley is kind of cute," Peter said, a little embarrassed.

"Eh, she's alright," Brady said, obviously committed to his crush, (and Peter's mother) Anna.

"Will she be at the party?" Peter asked.

"I would think so. Jane and she are friends," Brady replied, "and between you and me, Taylor told me she thinks you're kind of cute."

Peter smiled a little.

"I have no idea how she could think that," Brady added in a joking manner.

Peter laughed. He wished that he could see Taylor right now. He had never felt so strongly about a girl he had just met, other than Sarah, and unlike Sarah this girl thinks he is cute.

Peter loved being in the past. He was a different person. He was the "new kid" who had friends and wasn't just some "loser kid". He could actually talk with his dad and have fun with him without worrying about meeting his expectations. The past was looking sweeter and sweeter to Peter, and he completely forgot about his own time.

"So," Peter said, changing the conversation, "you like Anna?"

"Yeah, I'm crazy about her, but she can't stand me. I don't know what it is about her, but I just have to be with her, you know? I'm thinking about just giving up. I don't know though, it's hard," Brady confessed.

Peter and his father had never had this deep of a conversation before in their lives.

"Yeah, I understand, man," Peter agreed. "You can't give up though. You're a cool guy, and she will come around someday. I guarantee it."

"Thanks, Petey. You're an alright dude. Tomorrow you definitely got to come over and play me in FIFA. We will see how good you really are," Brady challenged.

"Sounds like a plan," Peter said.

Peter just had the longest and most intimate conversation he ever had with his dad that wasn't an argument. Why couldn't things be like this in Peter's own time? Why did his dad not have to be his dad in order for them to be close? Peter didn't understand but nonetheless enjoyed the quality time with his dad.

"Sorry, I've just been driving around…where am I taking you?" Brady asked.

"Just turn here," Peter directed, with no clue on where Brady was taking him.

Peter randomly said, *"Turn here,"* every few streets. Eventually, he told Brady to stop and pointed to a random house. Brady looked at Peter funny; the house was old with no lights on and no cars in the driveway. Peter opened the door of the car and slowly walked to the door of the house. He moved slow enough to make sure Brady left before he reached the door. Peter got to the doorstep. Once Brady drove off, Peter started to turn around while thinking of places he could stay the night. He then turned back around and faced the door. The door had a sign on it. The sign read:

Notice of Eviction

Bank agents will be here on MARCH 13th, 2012 to gain ownership of this house. Make sure all residents of this location will be gone by this date. This includes all people, pets, and other items that you would like to keep.

Peter thought for a little while, and read the sign over again. If the family left already, then couldn't he stay until March 13th?

Peter did the math in his head. *If today is Monday, March 5th, then wouldn't I have five days till the lottery drawing? No one will be at this house until the 13th. This gives a couple days to cash in my ticket.*

Peter then realized he had to make sure the family had moved out already. He knocked on the door. Then Peter waited five minutes and knocked again. He waited a while longer until he mustered up enough courage to try and open the door. Finally Peter reached out for the handle, grabbed it and it turned.

He opened the door and saw nothing. It was empty. He figured he could stay here long enough to get the lottery money. He began to figure out his living arrangements. He went upstairs and searched the house for something to sleep on. All he found was an old book and a dresser full of older clothes.

Peter took the book downstairs to where he was going to sleep. He laid down to read the book. He skimmed through the book and in one of the pages he found fifty dollars in cash, two twenty dollar bills and one ten dollar bill. Peter then realized that before now, he had no money. Peter was lucky he came across this cash. He figured it would be enough to last him until the lottery drawing. Peter then closed his eyes and went to sleep.

CHAPTER 8

Peter woke up the next day a little sore from sleeping on the floor. He went to the bathroom to see if the shower worked. Miraculously, it worked. Even though he didn't have any soap, the warm water felt soothing on his stiff neck.

Fortunately, he was able to find clothes to wear in the dresser. He looked through each drawer carefully and couldn't really find anything that he liked. He finally settled on a plain, white t-shirt, an old, blue Adidas warm-up jacket and some jeans. The jeans were a little big, but he found a belt to hold them up. He was surprised when the jacket fit him perfectly.

Peter walked out the backdoor so the neighbors didn't notice him. He started walking to school but when he was about half way to Trenton High School, Alex pulled up along side of him.

"You need a ride?" Alex asked Peter.

"Sure, thanks, man," Peter replied.

Alex's car wasn't as nice as Thomas's or Brady's, but at least it was a car. It had a brown exterior with some rust by the front wheels. He didn't have leather seats but it was cozy.

"So, you pumped about the half school day today?" Alex said to Peter excitedly.

"Half day? You guys have those?" Peter replied, confused.

"Yeah! And today is the only time of the year we have them on Tuesday, because of spring break this week!" Alex explained.

"So, spring break starts today after the half day? When does our break end?" Peter asked.

"We go back to school on Monday. We only have five and a half days for our break," Alex continued, showing disappointment with the school.

"Dang, so we practically have a week off?" Peter said.

"Yeah, pretty much," Alex replied to Peter. "Hey, Michael, Brady, Mitch, Thomas and I are going to Pizza Market after school today for some grub, you in?"

"Sure thing," Peter cheerfully agreed.

After school, Peter waited for Thomas out in the parking lot. While waiting for Thomas, Peter noticed Taylor approaching. Peter quickly matted his hair down with his hand.

"Hey, Peter!" Taylor said with a smile.

"Hey, Taylor," Peter greeted her, getting a little red in the face.

"I'm looking forward to tomorrow! And by the way, are you going to Jane's party Friday?" Taylor asked Peter.

"Oh, yeah, I'll be going. And what's tomorrow?" Peter asked.

"Our date? Thomas set us up…he didn't tell you?" Taylor asked, somewhat surprised.

"No, he failed to mention that," Peter said, a little mad at

Thomas for not telling him something so wonderful. "What's the plan for our date?"

"We can go to Trenton House…it's a nice local restaurant. Thomas said you can't drive, so I'll pick you up at six. Where should I pick you up at?" Taylor asked.

"Umm…" Peter tried to think of some landmark by his house. He then remembered he had seen a library next to it while he was waiting to go in. "My house is by the library. It's a white house with a blue door. Just knock…the doorbell doesn't work," Peter said.

"It's a date," Taylor said, smiling. "See you tomorrow."

"Bye, Taylor," Peter spoke with a goofy grin on his face.

Peter was floating on air right now. He, Peter Thompson, just scored a date with the prettiest sophomore in the whole school. Future Peter could never do that. He didn't realize that there was no difference between past and future Peter. He was just being himself, something he was afraid to do in his own time.

Peter then waited another two minutes for Thomas to arrive. He had a girl with him.

"Sorry, Peter…I had to go talk to Mrs. Lane about my test. Oh, and by the way, this is my girlfriend, Tiffany Lindemann," Thomas informed Peter, while gesturing to Tiffany.

"Hey, Peter, I've heard nothing but great things about you!" Tiffany said to Peter.

"Oh, I'm not that great," Peter sighed, being modest.

Tiffany smiled and they jumped into the car. Peter thought he should let Tiffany take the front seat so he climbed into the back seat.

Tiffany was tall with smooth skin. She had pretty green eyes, long, blonde hair, and a beautiful smile.

"Way to not tell me about my date with Taylor!" Peter spoke angrily to Thomas, once they started to drive.

"Oh, yeah, sorry, bud, I tend to forget things often," Thomas admitted.

"That's alright…at least I got the date," Peter said smiling.

They started heading to Pizza Market to meet up with the gang. Tiffany and Thomas talked most of the way there.

Peter just sat quietly in the back thinking about his upcoming date. He had never been on a date before. He didn't know what to do or what he was going to say. He went from being excited to scared to death. Peter was never good with women or even people for that matter. He knew she was out of his league and he just hoped he wouldn't screw it up. Peter thought about this the whole way and finally they arrived at Pizza Market.

As they climbed out of the car, they saw that Alex and Mitch just arrived. Brady and Michael were already inside waiting.

"Dude! Why'd you bring her along?" Alex asked Thomas.

"Yeah, now we can't talk about her and her friends behind their backs," Mitch chuckled in a joking way.

"Very funny, guys," Tiffany said picking up on the joke.

They laughed and walked into Pizza Market. Peter could already tell they were going to have a good time. These guys were very outgoing and hilarious. He wished he was more like that. Then he would have more friends. He was glad he had friends here that accepted him. All the more reason Peter wanted to stay.

They walked over to the table where Brady and Michael were sitting. They were already eating pizza.

"You guys better get you some pizza before we eat it all," Brady said.

They went to the counter and all bought lunch buffets. They grabbed their pizza and sat down.

"So where are your ladies at?" Tiffany asked the group.

"Beats me," Brady said, being a little upset with Tiffany because she knew what was going on between Anna and him.

Michael told her that his girlfriend Zoe was on vacation and Mitch's girlfriend, Megan was eating with her cousin who was visiting for spring break. Alex didn't have a girlfriend but the guys joked with him about being a huge flirt. Peter and the guys laughed. Alex didn't appreciate it but still gave a tiny chuckle.

"I should've invited Taylor...sorry, Peter," Tiffany apologized.

"It's alright, I'll see her tomorrow," Peter said.

"Oh? You will?" Brady, Alex, Michael, and Mitch asked Peter all at once.

"Yeah, Thomas set me up on a date," Peter admitted.

"Nice, dude. Where you guys going?" Brady asked.

"Some place called Trenton House," Peter replied.

"That's a nice place," Brady said. "Good luck, man."

"Thanks...I'll need it," Peter confessed, becoming nervous again.

They ate their pizza and talked about spring break and their plans. Peter had never had this much fun before. He had never gone to lunch with a big group. He had only really hung out with Tyler. Peter missed Tyler, but he loved his new friends. After they finished eating, they started piling in their cars and were going to head to Brady's house for some PS3.

"Gee, I love you, man…but she is not coming over," Brady warned Thomas.

"Sorry, Tiff, I gotta take you home," Thomas said a little upset.

"It's alright, see you guys Friday. Nice meeting you, Peter."

Thomas left to drop her off while the guys went to Brady's house. He lived in the North Land Acres. Peter had no idea that the North Land Acres had existed this long ago. It was a really nice neighborhood. They showed Peter where Jane's party was going to be, considering she also lived in the same neighborhood.

"You guys are staying the night, Thursday after the nuggets and Friday after the party, end of discussion," Brady said forcefully.

"Fair enough," the group responded.

Peter was glad he didn't have to stay in that cruddy house for a couple of nights.

The group went into Brady's basement and started up the PS3. Peter and Brady were going to have their grudge match. Peter was determined to win. He knew he would gain major respect from the gang. He also really wanted to earn his dad's approval, even if it was something as trivial as FIFA.

Brady chose team USA, while Peter decided to be Mexico. Therefore, the teams would be even.

Thomas arrived just before they started the game and it was on. Smack talk was flying all over the place. It was getting heated.

When Brady would score a goal, the guys would go crazy. Peter would answer right back and the guys would give Brady crap. It was the most intense FIFA match ever played. Peter had never played anyone this good before. He had to admit his dad had mad skills.

Peter, in extra time, scored the go-ahead goal to win the game. Peter had done it. Everyone in the room came at Brady with jokes and insults. Peter felt on top of the world. Brady was in shock. He told Peter he had played a good game, but just sat there stunned. The guys just kept raining praise on Peter, the greatest FIFA player ever.

Peter didn't know why these boys were so serious about video games, but he didn't mind the attention one bit. Brady knew he would never live it down. He had been beaten by the new kid.

After all the intensity, the gang relaxed and played a few more games, none of which were as intense as Peter and Brady's. Then they heard a noise. It was rain hitting Brady's roof.

"I'm going, guys, in case it storms," Alex spoke, seeming very concerned.

"Yeah, me, too," Mitch and Michael chimed.

They went to their cars and headed home. Thomas, Brady, and Peter were all alone now.

CHAPTER 9

"Crap, I just remembered I have to take these games back to Dootzy's," Thomas complained.

"What is Dootzy's?" Peter asked.

"It's a movie and game rental store. It's close to Dairy King," Brady replied.

"Oh, well, are you going to take me home on your way there?" Peter asked.

"What? Oh, we aren't driving, Petey, we are walking there," Thomas laughed.

"ARE YOU CRAZY? It's pouring outside!" Peter exclaimed.

"That's just the kind of crazy stuff we do around here, Pete-diggity. You have to learn to deal with it," Brady said while Thomas continued laughing.

"So, are you in or out?" Thomas questioned.

Peter thought about it. He never did crazy things like this. Now was his chance to be a part of one of his dad's "adventures."

"I'm in!" Peter shouted.

They geared up for the long trek. Don't think that this is just some short little walk down the street. This was probably a mile-long walk, and they were going to do it in the pouring rain. They wore hoodies, sweats, and hats. They didn't want to catch a cold before the game tomorrow. They started to walk down North Land Court, the street where Brady lived, and the adventure had begun.

After awhile they were on Third Street. Now this street was a nightmare for people walking. It seems like it goes on forever. It didn't help that it was pouring and very cold. Brady and Thomas were just talking and laughing and enjoying the adventure. Peter was nervous. He didn't know if it was going to storm or what. He was freezing and wet.

My dad is nuts! Peter thought.

Then all of a sudden a black car pulls up by them.

"Where you guys going?" asked the stranger.

"We are just heading to Dootzy's," Brady said perfectly calm.

"Oh, you guys want a ride?" the stranger asked.

"Sure," Peter said.

Thomas then punched Peter's arm.

"OW!"

"No, thanks, sir," Brady said.

"Are you sure?" asked the strange man.

"Yeah, we are fine. Thanks," Thomas assured him.

The man then made a U-turn and headed off.

"Wait, did that man just make a U-turn?" Brady asked.

"Yeah, he just went out of his way to pick us up," Thomas reasoned.

"He was just being nice by trying to give us a ride," Peter said.

Thomas and Brady busted up laughing.

"You are lucky we are here, amigo," Brady informed him.

They joked with Peter the whole way. Whether the stranger was bad or not, they liked messing with Peter.

Peter didn't realize that you weren't supposed to get into cars with strangers. He guessed that they just stopped teaching that to the youth sometime between 2012 and 2035.

They went to Dootzy's and returned the games. They stopped at Dairy King and told everyone there about the adventure. Everyone got a kick out of it and heckled Peter because he almost got inside a stranger's car.

After awhile Peter left and went to the house where he was staying. He remembered he had a huge date the next day. It then occurred to Peter to take the eviction sign off of the door. If Taylor would have seen that it would have blown his cover. Even though Peter was dog-tired, he was too nervous about his date that he had a hard time falling asleep that night.

Tomorrow was his first real date with a girl, and this girl was very popular and pretty. Peter was afraid of screwing up, and began thinking of every possible way he could ruin the date. After awhile, he became so tired that he finally managed to fall asleep.

CHAPTER 10

Peter slept in Wednesday morning. He was exhausted from the previous long day and from staying up late thinking about the date. Peter remembered the conversation he and Taylor had. She was picking him up at six o'clock. He realized he needed some nicer clothes. He only had $40 left, so he couldn't afford to buy clothes and pay for the date.

Peter decided to walk to Northland Acres and visit his dad. He would ask him for some clothes. He made the long walk and finally arrived. Peter knocked on the door and when Brady's mother answered, he realized this woman was his grandma.

Peter had never met his grandma. She became really sick right when his father graduated from high school, so his dad could not afford to go to college. Because Brady didn't get a college education, he only made just enough money to support his family. Peter was regarded as being poor in the future.

It was weird for Peter to meet his grandma. Considering he lived his whole life never knowing her, it was now, as a

15-year-old, that he was meeting her for the first time. He kept forgetting he was in the past.

Peter asked for Brady, and his grandma went and got him.

"What's up, Petey?" Brady asked.

"I need to borrow some nice clothes for my date tonight," Peter requested.

"You don't have anything nice to wear?" Brady said, not even noticing that Peter was still wearing the same shirt from yesterday.

"No, can you spot me some clothes?" Peter asked.

"Well, I guess I can help you out, you definitely need it," Brady said.

"Thanks, man," Peter said.

They went inside to Brady's room. His room was designed with a horseshoe type logo. Brady had a cardboard cut-out of some quarterback.

"What's with your room?" Peter asked.

"You don't know who the Indianapolis Colts are?" Brady said shocked.

"No, who are they?" Peter asked.

"Only the best football team ever; home to Peyton Manning, the best quarterback of all time," Brady bragged, somewhat dumbfounded that Peter didn't know this. "Geez, first Derrick Rose, now the Colts? Come on, Petey, you must start watching ESPN."

In Peter's time the Colts were not a football team. They were actually the Los Angeles Hurricanes then. They moved from Indianapolis to Los Angeles in 2023 and changed their name as well. Peter had heard of Peyton Manning before. When his dad made him watch sports with him he had heard

Peyton Manning's name mentioned. He actually did go down as the best quarterback of all time. He didn't realize his dad had loved them so much as a kid.

"Oh, that's awesome, I don't really watch much football," Peter admitted.

"WHAT? You're crazy, man!" Brady exclaimed.

"Sorry," Peter said.

"Don't apologize. It's all good, man," Brady then calmly spoke.

Wow, Peter thought, *my dad, as a kid, doesn't make me be like him.*

Peter liked his dad in the past. They got along well, and did things together. Something Peter and his dad never did in the future. Brady grabbed some clothes for Peter. They were a little big considering Brady was 6'4" and Peter was only 6'0". It would work though. Peter took the clothes and headed back home.

But before Peter left, Brady had one last thing to say.

"Hey, man, just stay calm on your date, be yourself, you're a cool dude," he said.

This made Peter love the past even more than the present; his dad just straight-up said Peter was cool.

"Thanks, man," Peter said. "Oh, and good luck with the first round of state tonight… hope you guys win."

He had checked the time before he left. It was 4 o'clock. He arrived home, showered, changed, and then just waited for Taylor. He started to have nerves. He didn't know what was going to happen. After playing the date over and over in his head, he heard a knock. This was it. He opened the door and his jaw dropped. Peter was stunned at the way Taylor looked.

"Wow…you look…" Peter managed to spit out.

"What do you think?" Taylor said, smiling. She then twirled around to show off her blue skirt and her silky, white blouse.

Well, that was just the cutest thing I've ever seen, Peter thought.

"You look amazing," Peter told her, finishing his thought.

"Come on, Peter, stop staring and let's go," Taylor said, joking with Peter.

Peter and Taylor started walking to her car. Taylor's car was pretty nice; it was small, and blue. Peter was a gentleman and went around to the driver's side door and opened it for Taylor. She smiled and thanked him. Then Peter went to get into the passenger's seat.

"I always imagined I'd be the one driving on my first date, not sitting in the passenger's seat," Peter confessed.

"This is your first date?" Taylor said, ignoring the driver comment.

"Well, yeah…but I'm glad I get to spend it with you," Peter admitted.

"I'm sure glad, too," Taylor responded.

After that, they continued on with conversation talking about this and that. Finally, Taylor pulled in front of a small, white building with a red sign reading *Trenton House.* Peter and Taylor walked in, with Peter holding the door, of course. Inside it was dark, with dimmed lights, and it was crowded. The waitress seated them in the back corner.

"So, what's the best thing to order here?" Peter asked Taylor.

"I know this might sound childish, but I'm a chicken tenders kind-of-person," Taylor suggested.

"Two orders of chicken tenders, it is," Peter said.

That's exactly what Peter told the waitress when she came to take their order. It took about 10 minutes for their food to come out. Peter made sure he didn't eat too fast; he did not want to seem like a pig.

Peter then thought, *Wow, this date is going great!*

After they were done eating, and Peter paid for the food, he asked Taylor what she wanted to do next.

"I don't know, we could go hang out at my house, or we could go see a movie or something?" Taylor replied.

They decided to go see a movie. It seemed like forever before they arrived at the theatre. It had to be about a 25 minute drive. In Peter's time they had a movie theatre right in the center of town. As they were standing in line to buy tickets, Peter pulled out his money.

"Oh, no, Peter, I got the tickets," Taylor insisted. "You paid for dinner."

"No, it's all good," Peter declared.

Peter handed the lady a twenty after having Taylor pick the movie. She chose *Chainsaw Death Wish*. Peter did not mind scary movies. He actually found them funny, especially those made before 2020. He always thought the effects are terrible so he made fun of them. Peter told himself he wouldn't make fun of this movie, nevertheless, he will be laughing in his mind.

Peter and Taylor found their seats. They were sitting in front of two guys who seemed to be about their same age. Peter then told Taylor he was going to get snacks. When he turned back to look at Taylor, before he walked out of the theatre, he noticed one of the guys behind her was glaring at him. Peter shook it off and went to the concession stand. He ordered popcorn and two Cokes. He brought the food back to where

Taylor was sitting. She was talking to the guy that was staring at Peter. She did not seem interested in him. Peter walked up and completely interrupted the conversation.

"Here you go, Taylor," Peter said while handing her the popcorn and a Coke.

"Thanks, Peter, you're a true gentleman," she emphasized to him, obviously hinting this at the guy behind them.

This is when the kid behind them butted in.

"Taylor, who is this clown?" he asked.

"The name's Peter, nice to meet you," Peter said sarcastically, sticking out his hand toward the kid.

"Oh, we've got a funny guy on our hands," the guy quipped.

"Greg, shut up and mind your own business," Taylor said to him, obviously displeased with Greg.

Greg was an extremely buff guy. He had acne and was about 5 foot 5 inches, very short for a guy.

"What, are you guys on a date or something?" Greg said to Taylor with an "are you serious?" look on his face.

"Yeah, and it's the best date I've ever been on!" she replied.

"Oh, yeah, and our date last month wasn't great?" Greg asked of Taylor.

"Yeah, that date pretty much sucked," Taylor grumbled.

"Whatever," Greg mumbled.

Then he directed his attention towards Peter.

"Hey, man, you think you got a chance with her? Well you don't! She will be mine again soon…so back off!"

This got Peter angry. He didn't realize that all girls come with baggage. Sometimes you find a girl worth overlooking her baggage. Now, Taylor was Peter's girl.

"Okay, listen here, buddy, obviously she doesn't like you, and I don't think any girl with some sort of self-respect or a decent taste in men will like you anytime soon. So why don't you just get out of here and leave us to our date," Peter said firmly to Greg .

Greg swung at Peter. Peter quickly ducked out of the way of the punch. Greg, obviously unhappy with his first attempt to hurt Peter, decided to hold off his anger. Greg and his friend left the movie.

"Wow, Peter, that was so nice of you to get rid of him," Taylor complimented.

"Eh, don't mention it, but he's pretty much the biggest tool I've ever met. By the way, can you please explain what your history with that guy is?" Peter questioned.

"I will after the movie," Taylor agreed.

Peter just realized the movie had started already. They both sat down. Taylor then leaned over closer to Peter.

"Thanks for getting rid of him…you're so sweet," Taylor whispered in a soft, tender voice.

Taylor then kissed Peter on the cheek. This was probably the most exciting moment of his life. He just got kissed on the cheek! Peter was excited beyond all means.

The rest of the movie was good as well. After the kiss, Peter and Taylor held hands the whole movie. With every creepy or suspenseful moment in the movie, Taylor would bury her head in Peter's shoulder. After the movie was done, they walked out to Taylor's car. They climbed in and started talking about the whole Greg incident.

Peter found out that Taylor and Greg had dated for awhile about a month ago. Taylor broke up with him because she realized he was stuck-up and mean. Peter understood why

Taylor was so happy he chased Greg away. He would have ruined Taylor's whole night.

Taylor then took Peter home. Once they got to Peter's house, Taylor and Peter started talking again.

"I had a great time tonight, Peter," she said.

"I did too…it was awesome!" Peter said smiling.

"So, I'll see you at the party?" Taylor asked.

"Yes, definitely," Peter assured her.

"Awesome, see you there," Taylor smiled and then left.

Peter returned her smile and then turned around to go back to his house. He walked in and just passed out on the floor, worn out from his date. The kiss on the cheek he had received was the last thought that crossed his mind before he fell asleep with a big smile on his face.

CHAPTER 11

Peter woke up the next day feeling amazing. He went to take a shower and change. Shortly after he was dressed, Peter heard a car honking right outside his house. He looked out the window. It was Thomas's car. Brady was hanging out of the sun-roof yelling for Peter. He could see that people were in the backseat, too. Peter ran downstairs and out to the car. He opened up the door to the backseat to find that they left him the middle seat, right between Michael and Alex.

"What are you guys doing here?" Peter asked. "Where's Mitch?"

"We won, Peter! We won last night!" Alex said. "Oh, and he had to mow the lawn."

"Oh, nice. Well, sorry I couldn't be there. I was on a date with Taylor," Peter boasted, but sad that he missed their game.

"Oh, nice, dude, but you aren't gonna miss it when we win state, right?" Michael said.

"I'll be there…I don't know how I'm going to get all the way up to Peoria. But I'll do my best," Peter responded.

"Maybe Taylor will take you," Thomas said jokingly from the driver's seat.

"Oh, ha-ha, but maybe she will," Peter quipped back to Thomas.

"You're a goofball, Pete-diggity," Brady said.

"NUGGETS!" Alex said out of the blue.

"Oh, yeah, tonight's when we are eating a bunch of nuggets. Are you still in, Petey?" Brady asked.

"Sure," Peter answered.

"Alright, Peter, hop in the back seat and let's go!" Thomas said.

Peter hopped over Michael and plopped down in the middle seat.

"So, where are we going?" Peter asked.

"MINI-PUTT!" Alex yelled.

"Gosh, dang it, Alex, it's like 40 degrees outside," Michael said.

"MINI-PUTT!" Alex repeated.

"Fine, you convinced me," Michael reluctantly agreed.

"Mini-Putt, is it?" Thomas then asked everyone in the car.

"MINI-PUTT!" everyone yelled.

Thomas then turned onto the highway and they were off. About 20 minutes later they arrived at a place called "Centerfield Mini-Golf." Everyone scrambled out of the car and ran to the ticket booth. Thomas said that he just cashed his paycheck so he would pay for everyone. They all received their putters and their golf balls and walked to the first hole.

"This ten dollar bill says that I win today," Thomas said to everyone.

"Okay, I'll take that bet," Peter challenged.

"Alright, Petey is gonna take me on...this kid is crazy," Thomas said.

"Dang, Peter, you're insane, cause Thomas is the best player on the Wesclin Golf Team," Alex informed him.

Peter then realized he had made a mistake, but it really didn't matter, for Peter was going to have fun with his friends. Halfway through the round, Thomas was up eight strokes on Peter. Peter was six over par and Thomas was two under par. Peter knew he was going to lose. Peter was actually doing the worst in the group, with Brady one over par, Michael three over par, and Alex five over. When they finally got to the last hole, the standings were the same. Thomas was now six under par, Brady was three under par, Michael was one over par, Alex was still five over, and Peter was in last place at seven over now.

"You ready to pay up, Peter?" Thomas asked.

"Hey, how bout you give Peter a chance to still win this thing? If he strokes a hole-in-one on this hole, he wins," Alex chirped in.

"Alright, that's fair," Thomas said, confident that Peter would not hole-in-one this hole.

Peter set his ball down and just went for it. There were a lot of obstacles, rocks, and hills in the way. Peter had no idea how he was going to make it, but he had to. He couldn't afford to lose ten dollars. He just hit the ball straight and hoped for the best. It bounced off of a rock, over a hill, went into a little divot that brought it around another rock and it headed straight for the hole. It was going to be close. Peter's ball stopped right on the edge of the hole.

"Go, ball!" Michael yelled at the ball.

Magically, with Michael's command, the ball rolled in. It was a hole-in-one! Everyone went crazy. Peter just made a miracle putt to win ten dollars. Since Peter had entered the past, his new group of friends have been amazed by him. He liked being somebody instead of a nobody like he was in his own time.

The rest of the day flew by fast. After mini-putt they all went to Brady's. Mitch was done mowing the lawn, so he came over too. Finally it was 11:30 at night and the gang went to McDonald's and bought 200 chicken nuggets for the six of them.

After picking up the ridiculous order of nuggets, they went back to Brady's house. It was going to be a historic night. They sat down at Brady's dinner table and began to chow down. They were stuffing their faces while still enjoying the incredible Chicken McNuggets from McDonald's.

They talked and laughed while they ate. Alex showed everyone his food in his mouth and the group laughed and said he was disgusting. After awhile the gang was slowing down. Mike couldn't take it anymore, his arms were plain tired. With the loss of the use of his arms, he had to eat nuggets without his hands.

It appeared the nuggets were going to win. Mitch was having a hard time with his nuggets. Brady was leading the group. Peter was holding his own and still eating at a steady pace. There were twenty nuggets left. The group was reluctant to eat anymore.

This is my chance, Peter thought. *I could really prove myself to these guys.*

Peter grabbed a nugget. The group didn't know what was going on. He kept grabbing more and more nuggets. After eating about 30 nuggets already, he had managed to eat 20 more. Peter had eaten 50 whole Chicken McNuggets. It was unheard of.

"You're nutty, Petey!" Alex said.

"Yeah, man, you're gonna explode!" said Thomas.

"Ugh…" Peter said immediately regretting his decision.

"You're alright, Petey. You're officially one of us now," Brady said.

Peter had just been accepted for who he is by his dad. It made his stomach feel a little better. The group was ecstatic that they had accomplished such a feat. They joked with Mitch, saying they were going to kick him out of the group because he only ate six nuggets. Whether or not he actually ate six they didn't know. They went to the basement recapping the event that had just occurred. Brady grabbed his guitar.

"We gotta write a song about this," he said.

"Yeah, true, then let's do it," Thomas said.

Brady started playing some chords. Then he put some lyrics with it. In about five minutes, Brady had written a song that portrayed the greatness of the nugget challenge. This is how it went.

"We went to McDonald's and we got 200 nuggets.
Mitch ate like six, Peter ate like 50.
Michael lost use of his arms and he ate like an animal.
And Alex grossed everyone out when he showed us all his food.
I felt like I was gonna throw up.
I felt like I was gonna throw up."

Then he broke off into a miraculous guitar solo with his voice and the group busted up laughing. They called up some girls and serenaded them with the song. The girls just laughed and said they loved it. They were mesmerized by Peter eating 50 nuggets. The group sang and laughed most of night.

Peter was amazed at how skilled his father was, even if the song was stupid. He appreciated getting mentioned in the song. He will always be remembered as the new kid who ate 50 McNuggets.

They finally called it quits and laid down. Peter then remembered tomorrow was Jane's party. He liked the idea that he was going to see Taylor again.

Peter woke up to lots of laughter. At first, Peter was confused, thinking it was already morning. Peter then realized it was still the middle of the night, and Thomas, Brady, and Michael were still awake.

"Aye! Pete is up!" Thomas yelled, still laughing.

"What are you guys laughing about? And what time is it?" Peter responded, a little crabby from being suddenly awakened.

"It's three in the morning, and we are looking at Alex's phone. That's why we're laughing. He's a huge flirt," Brady said.

"He's got game," Michael added.

"He was texting like three girls yesterday," Thomas said.

"Gosh dang it, Alex," Michael said while sticking his hand in a bag of chips. "He was texting Kate, Miranda, and Bianca."

They all continued late night conversation for a while until they were interrupted by Alex himself.

"Get out of here, Leopold!" the sleeping Alex said randomly.

"Who's Leopold?" Thomas asked Alex, then turned to Brady and whispered "I hope he's sleep talking again."

Brady laughed and then said, "Me too, that's hilarious."

"Apparently I ordered the poop sandwich!" Alex spouted with an irritated voice.

Michael, Brady, Thomas, and Peter all looked at each other and immediately started laughing their heads off.

"This dude is insane!" Michael said about Alex, while laughing.

They all laughed for another five minutes straight before continuing their conversation again. The guys told Peter the stories of other times Alex has sleep-talked, including the time he admitted his feelings for Michael's girlfriend.

Peter then stayed up talking with the guys that were still up. He was surprised they didn't wake up Mitch and Alex with the laughter like they woke up Peter. About 15 minutes later, they all drifted asleep.

They woke up the next morning at around 10 o'clock. They got dressed and ready for the day and then decided to go out to breakfast. They all picked up some Casey's gas station breakfast pizza. Then everyone went to hangout at Thomas's house. They played some video games for a while and before they knew it, it was 4 PM.

CHAPTER 12

Thomas and Brady needed to head over to Jane's house to set up. Peter had completely forgotten that his dad's band was playing at this party! Peter could not decide what he was looking forward to more, seeing Taylor, or seeing his dad's band. Peter was getting excited.

The group left Thomas's house and they went to Jane's to help the band set up. The whole group knocked on Jane's door. She answered and greeted them warmly. Jane gave Peter a strange look. He couldn't decide if it was a *Who is this kid?* or an *Oh man, who is this cutie?* Either way, Peter just followed Brady downstairs.

Peter was amazed by this basement. It had a hardwood floor and a nice living room area with an enormous TV. The hardwood floor area was huge and empty which made for a great dance floor, and there was a stage by the back wall. Jane also had a table set up for snacks and drinks, and there was a pool table by the TV. This party was going to be awesome.

Peter asked Thomas, who was carrying a huge amplifier,

what he could do. Thomas told him that he could bring in the lights. Peter went out to Thomas's car and looked in the trunk. Inside, there was a cardboard box labeled "LIGHTS", so Peter assumed these were it. When Peter brought the stuff down, the stage was looking legit. Amps, speakers, and chords on the floor covered the stage. Plus, there was Thomas's huge drum set located in the center of the back of the stage.

Thomas then walked downstairs from another trip to his car to get the guitars they would be using. He had three cases in his hands.

"Geez, Brady, got enough guitars?" Thomas asked, while struggling to hold up the cases.

"Sorry, dude, I want to have variety tonight," Brady advised.

Thomas then brought down a keyboard and an acoustic guitar. After about an hour of setting up, the stage looked perfect. It looked very professional. Thomas had a tech board and a laptop computer by his drum set so he could control the lights and sounds.

Wow, this is an impressive gig for two people, Peter thought.

Finally, Thomas and Brady got a ladder and hung up a banner over the stage that read "UP TO KNOW GOOD."

Peter was getting anxious to watch them play. It seemed like Brady and Thomas weren't nervous at all. Peter knew he would be nervous, playing for practically the whole high school at the party-of-the-year. Peter heard Alex ask Jane how many people were expected to show up and she said around 250! Her house, though, definitely had room for them.

About 20 minutes before the party officially started, Up To Know Good began to warm up. Thomas was pulling off some basic beats to warm up while Brady was tuning his guitars. They were making sure the sounds were working on each amp and checking all the lights.

Then finally, Thomas counted four stick hits and they started playing a warm-up song. Peter didn't recognize the song; nevertheless it had some nice drums and a sweet guitar part. Brady wasn't singing during the warm-up though. It seemed like that song was over too soon, but Peter was ready for the party to start.

Peter had never really been to a party, especially one like this. Once the clock hit six, people were rushing in the doors going straight to the pool table, the snack table, the TV, or to get a good dancing spot in front of the stage.

At about 6:15 PM Brady spoke into the microphone and said that they'd be starting in five minutes. Everyone that was on a couch or talking somewhere else immediately went to the stage to get ready.

Peter was talking to Alex, Michael, and Mitch when a soft, gentle hand grabbed his arm.

"Let's dance!" Taylor begged of Peter with a smile.

Peter grinned back and matted his hair down. Then they walked to the dancing area. The area was already getting filled with people anxiously awaiting the band to start playing.

Peter and Taylor talked for a little bit and then were silenced by the lights going out. The whole place was completely dark. Peter felt Taylor grab his hand. Then out of no where, everyone heard a guitar melody which was haunting and beautiful.

Cheers erupted from the crowd. To be heard over the crowd, Taylor told Peter that the song they were playing was called "The Pretender" by The Foo Fighters. Peter started to cheer along.

Then Peter heard his dad's voice...it was a very strong voice. Peter wondered why he hadn't inherited his dad's traits and musical talents.

Suddenly, Peter heard the drums, accenting the whole song already. The way the band arranged these songs was brilliant. Then the lights came back on the stage, and you could see the band clearly now. Brady dressed in jeans and a sleeveless shirt, while Thomas wore jeans and a plaid, flannel shirt, sleeves rolled up to the elbows.

Peter then turned to Taylor and started dancing with her. He had some sense of rhythm to keep up with her moves, but she was a good dancer.

Peter was having the time of his life, and he thought it was fantastic. He was living in the past, practically best friends with his dad and his dad's friends. He was also dancing with a beautiful girl while listening to his dad's band play LIVE!

Then Peter remembered the lottery ticket. He actually stopped dancing to check his pocket to see if it was still there. Peter had been keeping it on him at all times while he was in the past. He sighed a sigh of relief when he felt it, then continued dancing. Peter then realized, on top of all of these wonderful things happening to him, he was also going to be a multi-millionaire soon. He couldn't help but smile as he started dancing closer to Taylor.

Three songs after the opener, everyone was still dancing strong. Brady announced on the microphone and informed everyone that they would now be playing a slow song. Therefore, everyone should grab a partner for a slow dance. Brady introduced the song and told everyone he would be playing acoustic and Thomas would be playing keyboard.

Thomas played a very impressive melody on the piano and then Brady accompanied him on guitar and vocals.

"I love this song," Taylor loudly spoke into Peter's ear so he could hear over the crowd.

"I've never heard it," Peter replied.

"You've never heard "Thousand Miles" by Vanessa Carlton?" Taylor asked, in shock.

"They slowed it down a lot, but it's a really good song."

"Oh, well, may I have this dance?" Peter asked politely in a formal tone.

"Why, yes! Yes, you may," Taylor responded with a gorgeous smile.

Peter grabbed her around her waist and she wrapped her arms around his shoulders. They were dancing pretty close. Peter thought this would be a good time to talk to Taylor about some stuff, but before he could even say anything, Thomas's girlfriend, Tiffany, walked up and whispered something to her. And like that, Taylor apologized and said she had to go upstairs for a little while to talk with her "broken-hearted and recently dumped" friend. Taylor was gone in an instant.

Peter started to walk over to the snack table to get a drink and was approached by Jane Brown.

"Taylor's leaving?" Jane asked.

"She's just going to talk to her friend," Peter said, unsure about Jane.

Jane had long brown hair and braces, with bright green eyes. Peter didn't really know anything about her.

"Oh, well, me and Taylor are really good friends. I'm sure she wouldn't mind if I took her dance, right?" Jane said in a flirty manner.

"Uh…well… I don't know…I kind of just want some lemonade," Peter said, very hesitantly.

"Oh, she won't mind!" Jane said and grabbed Peter's hand and led him to the dance floor.

By this time, the slow song was over, and Up to Know Good was back to playing their rock and roll. Jane grabbed Peter and started to dance, so close, she was almost on him. Peter felt very uncomfortable. Jane continued shaking her hips and dancing close to Peter. Peter looked to his right, and saw Taylor. She was staring right at them. Peter looked back over at Taylor. She was running up the stairs. He pushed Jane away from him and went up the stairs after Taylor. He saw the door leading outside closing. He opened it back up and went outside to find Taylor sitting on a hammock by Jane's pool. She was crying. Peter started to approach her.

"Why don't you just go back and dance with Jane?" Taylor said sobbing.

"Taylor, it wasn't what it looked like," Peter said.

He felt terrible; he had never made a girl cry.

"Oh, so she wasn't dancing all over you?" Taylor asked in a sarcastic tone while wiping her teary eyes.

"Yeah, she was, but it's not like I wanted her to," Peter said trying to get Taylor to believe him.

"Yeah, right, I couldn't leave you alone for ten minutes," Taylor wept.

"Look, Taylor, I didn't want her to dance with me. I tried to tell her no but she wouldn't listen. I like you, not her," Peter said, a little angry.

"Why should I believe you?" Taylor asked.

"Because I wouldn't lie to you. I think you're awesome, Taylor. Believe me; I really like you a lot."

"Really?" she asked, cheering up a little.

"Yes," Peter said.

"Well, I like you, too," Taylor joyfully spoke.

Peter had the biggest smile on his face. For once, the prettiest girl in school liked him.

"There room for one more?" Peter asked hopefully.

"Sure," she said happily and made room.

They laid on the hammock together and looked up at the stars. Then Peter saw the most amazing thing he had ever seen. It was the Big Dipper. It was shining so bright it was absolutely beautiful just like his mom described it.

"That's incredible," Peter said.

"I know. Every night you can see the Big Dipper in the night sky. Tonight it looks breathtaking," Taylor agreed.

"Funny, I was thinking the same about you," Peter said smoothly.

"You're a dork," Taylor said laughing.

Peter smiled, then said, "I'm really glad I met you, Taylor."

"Me too, you're a pretty cool kid," she said.

"That's the first time I've ever been called cool," he said. "At my old school I was kind of a loser."

"Well, you're very, very..." Taylor said this as she grabbed Peter's arm and made him put it around her, then she leaned her head on his shoulder, "very cool," she continued.

Peter grinned like a little boy in a candy shop. Peter then realized his whole "being from the future problem."

Peter stayed looking at the stars, and he still had his arm around Taylor. Taylor looked at Peter and noticed a sign of worry and stress on his face.

"What's wrong?" Taylor asked.

"Nothing…it's nothing," Peter said.

"No, tell me!" Taylor teased in a playful manner, assuming it was nothing very serious.

"Okay!"

Peter thought very long before deciding it was the right time to tell her his secret.

"You're not going to believe me."

"Yes, I will. It could be the most ridiculous thing in the world, and I'll believe you," Taylor said, assuring Peter.

"Okay, well, this is going to sound crazy," Peter began.

He got a huge knot in his stomach. This could ruin his whole relationship with Taylor.

"I'm from the future…I don't really know why I'm here. In my time, 2035, I'm a loser. No girls like you would ever like me, and I have a terrible relationship with my dad, too," Peter said very quickly. Before Taylor could respond, he went off again.

"The reason I wished to visit the past was to submit this winning lottery ticket. Tomorrow this ticket…"Peter pulled out the ticket, "will win me millions of dollars. I was planning to take it back to my time and become rich. However, on top of not knowing how to get back, I don't really want to go back. Here I have you and amazing friends and my dad actually likes me here. I am popular and live a good life."

"Your dad is here?" Taylor asked this question out of all the possible questions she could have.

"Brady is my dad…" Peter said, realizing how weird this would sound to Taylor. "I know this all seems unreal, but it isn't, and I don't know what to do about it."

"If this is all real, Peter, go back home, go back to your family, live the life you were meant to live…and as much as I hate to say this…you need to go back. You don't belong in this time," Taylor said honestly.

"I don't know how to go back…" Peter said, realizing the dilemma he had created for himself.

Everything that Taylor just said made sense. Who knows what this Peter living in the past could do to the future? He could make one false move and affect the entire future. Also, he realized that he was not meant to live in 2012.

"Well, how did you get here?" Taylor curiously asked.

"I know this sounds generic, but I wished upon a shooting star," Peter laughed at the idea of this.

"Well, then the next time you see a shooting star, wish to go back to your own time," Taylor suggested, like this was the obvious thing to do.

Peter never thought of that.

"I don't know. I bet Tyler misses me a lot."

"Tyler?" Taylor asked.

"He's my best friend," Peter said.

Taylor smiled at this. Then turned to Peter and asked him an honest question.

"Am I in the future at all?" Taylor asked.

"Oh, yeah, you are. You're actually a family friend, you used to live next to me, but I know your daughter, her name is Sarah," Peter said, like it was no big deal.

"I've always loved the name Sarah!" Taylor exclaimed.

"I have a crush on her," Peter said.

Peter and Taylor laughed at this for a while.

"Peter, if you leave, I'm going to miss you a lot. In case you do decide to leave…" Taylor said, while leaning closer to Peter. Peter turned his head. Taylor and Peter's lips connected.

Peter and Taylor kissed for a long time, pretty much the

rest of the time they spent on the hammock. Then Taylor got a phone call from her mom saying she had to come home. Taylor kissed Peter good-bye and then ran off.

Peter stayed lying out on the hammock for a long time. Then he heard someone calling his name, it was the crew, including Thomas and Brady.

"Over here!" Peter shouted.

"What's up, Petey? Whatcha doing out here alone?" Brady asked. Brady and Thomas were sweaty from their performance.

"Taylor was out here, she left about 30 minutes ago," Peter replied.

"Oh, I see, were you getting your lips a workout?" Thomas asked.

Peter just smiled and then asked, "So you guys are done playing?"

"Yeah, you missed it. We closed with our own original song, *See You Again.*"

"Oh, man, sorry I missed out," Peter apologized.

"It's okay, man, you were getting macked on…it's no biggie," Brady said.

Peter looked up at the night sky. The moon looked so big and bright; it was never this bright or big back in Peter's time.

"You guys should write a song about the moon," Peter said randomly.

"Peter, you're ridiculous. That's a crazy idea. What song is about the moon?" Thomas asked.

"Yours will be the first, if you write it!" Peter exclaimed.

"And you guys think that *I* say ridiculous things!" Alex stated.

Peter thought the whole moon song idea was good. Peter guessed he and his dad couldn't agree on everything, even in the past.

"Come on, Peter, let's bounce! We got a buncha food waiting at Brady's house for us," Michael said.

Peter plopped out of the hammock and followed them to the car. They all piled in and drove off to Brady's house. Since Brady lived in the neighborhood of Jane and Thomas, it was a short drive.

After they unloaded the sound and lights and stage equipment from the back, they went on inside. Peter's head was really spinning. Taylor said he should go back, but he didn't know if he wanted to. He had received his first kiss from an awesome girl and he has a lot of friends. Peter knew it was probably best to go back, but how was he going to pass up on the amazing life he has in the past and becoming a millionaire? He knew that if the time came, and a shooting star zoomed into the night sky, he would have to make a decision.

The crew just sat around and talked the whole night. They snacked, played some video games, joked around, and before they knew it, they were all asleep.

CHAPTER 13

Once Peter woke up, his head was still spinning. Peter grabbed a bottle of water from Brady's refrigerator and sat down on the couch.

About 15 minutes later, Alex and Michael woke up, shortly followed by Mitch and Brady, then finally Thomas. Brady decided that everyone should go home to get ready for the game tonight.

Brady called Taylor and asked her if she could give Peter a ride to the game that night. She said yes excitedly and hung up.

Alex gave Peter a ride home. As he went inside his empty home, he saw lying on the counter the eviction sign that was originally on the door. They were coming soon to take the house over. Peter really needed this money and had to think of a good way to win it.

If Peter won the money, he could buy a house in the past (if he were to stay) or even take the money back to the future with him and make his family rich. He could buy clothes, food, and actually live in the past instead of pretending to live in this lame house.

Peter then thought of something. He would have to find a trustworthy adult. No realtor is going to sell a house to a 15-year-old boy. No lottery company is going to give a 15-year-old boy 100 million dollars. Heck, no town is going to let a 15-year-old boy live by himself. He would need to find an adult to pretend to be his parent, buy his house, and cash in the lottery ticket as soon as possible. He thought of his friends' parents, they would all misunderstand. But he could try Brady's mom, which would also be his grandmother, but he might screw something up and mess up his great relationship with his father.

After thinking all day, Peter decided that he would first win the lottery, then tell his friends about it. They would all freak out and go crazy, and then Peter would tell them his parents left for a trip, so he had no one to cash it in. He was sure one of them would volunteer to get their parent to do it, but they would also have to buy Peter a house. They would most likely ask Peter why he needed a house, and he would say because he wants to surprise his parents when they get back from their "trip."

This whole idea to Peter seemed crazy, especially because his actual parents are his age. He thought it would probably work. But this plan was only if Peter decided to stay in the past. Peter was most likely leaning towards staying, but he really didn't know.

Peter checked the clock. It was 3:00 PM. Only two hours till the lottery drawing. He really didn't have to watch, he just had to wait till anytime after 5:00 PM. Then he could claim his lottery ticket won.

Taylor was picking him up at 5:00 as well. Eventually he heard Taylor outside the house. He walked out the door and leaped into her car.

"Look who's 100 million dollars richer!" Peter said, sarcastically, because they both knew he won.

"Oh nice! But you better cash that in quickly…a shooting star could happen anytime soon!" Taylor said jokingly, but she was serious.

"Yeah, yeah, let's just get to the game. I want to watch my dad win state!" Peter said excitedly.

"So I assume they're going to win?" Taylor concluded.

It seemed like the whole future thing was settling into their relationship. Taylor really did take it all extremely well. Almost anyone would freak out at the news that their boyfriend is from the future, if they even believed him. Nevertheless, Taylor kept her cool and believed him entirely.

After about a two hour car drive, they finally ended up in Peoria. It was an extremely long car drive, but Peter and Taylor flirted and joked the whole time.

They entered the stadium just in time to hear the announcing of the starting line-ups. Peter and Taylor found their seats. They were very nice seats right by the court. Sitting around them were all the students from THS that decided to travel north to see the team play.

And the starting line-up for the Carbondale Terriers—
Starting at Guard… number 17… Paul Pippets
Starting at the other Guard… number 11… Terry Jansen
Starting at Forward… number 30… Kevin Roche
Starting at the other Forward… number 1…Kevin Rock
And finally, starting at center…number 21… LaMichael Hill

Carbondale came out one by one, to the sound of their names. Each player looked better and better as they ran out onto the court. LaMichael Hill looked the most intimidating. He was a dark-skinned, tall, beefy kid. He had to be at least 6 foot 8 inches tall.

Taylor and Peter stood up along with all of the other Trenton fans when they started announcing the players.

And now…the starting line-up for the Trenton Warriors---
Starting at Guard… number 14… Alex Moore

Alex came running out and chest-bumped one of the other Trenton players. Alex looked very small compared to Carbondale's players.

Starting at the other Guard… number 23… Michael Johnson

Michael came running out and did the same as Alex. He shook hands with the opposing coach as well. Michael looked about the same size as the Paul Pippets for Carbondale.

And at forward…number 19… Mitch Williams

Mitch followed what Michael and Alex did before. Peter just realized how cool it was that the five best friends were also the starting five for the basketball team. Back in Peter's time, his dad would always talk about the starting five, but Peter just realized it really was special that they were all so talented together.

At the other forward… number 4… Thomas Jones

Everyone in the student section gave a big cheer for Thomas. They cheered for everyone else, too, but Peter thought Thomas's performance in the first game of state gave them a good player to look for in the finals. Thomas gave the chest bump, but he stayed in the middle of the court. It was sort of weird, like he was up to something.

And finally, at center…number 33… Brady Thompson

Cheers erupted and Peter's father came running onto the

court. He ran straight to Thomas and did a special handshake with him, a secret one. They then gathered the starting five and shared a special prayer. The team then did some sort of warm up. The game was finally going to start. The teams gathered at center court ready for the tip off.

The first play went like this; Thomas passed the ball to Alex to take it down the floor. Alex passed the ball around to every player. Then Thomas threw the ball up to the basket. The shot looked off. Then the crowd realized it wasn't a shot. Brady caught the ball in mid-air and threw up a breath-taking slam dunk.

Peter was in shock, because he didn't know his dad could dunk. His dad talked over and over about basketball, but never said he could dunk.

The first half ended with a tie game. The play was intense, the teams answering each other's baskets. Peter wasn't nervous because he knew the outcome. Taylor did too, yet she was still nervous. Brady would make the game winning shot and that would be it.

The second half of the game began, and the teams picked up where they left off. Peter didn't normally like basketball, but he was into the game. The fourth quarter came around and the Warriors were down by four. Peter knew that the Warriors were supposed to win, he just didn't know if the outcome would turn out like it should. Maybe Peter messed something up and he changed the outcome of the game by being there. He had never thought of the consequences of being in the past. Peter just hoped for the best.

With half of the fourth quarter over, Trenton was still down four points. Thomas hit a jump shot and they were now only down by two points.

With one minute left in the game, Trenton had the ball

when Alex took it down court. He passed it inside to Brady, who passed it back out to Thomas, who took a three-point attempt...SWISH! The ball went in. The crowd erupted, at least the Trenton fans did.

Hugs were going around the student section. Fans were so happy that they had taken the lead now.

Peter saw Tiffany, Thomas's girlfriend, going crazy; she was wearing all orange and black paint on her face and one of Thomas's jerseys. She was screaming "THAT'S MY BOYFRIEND!" while hugging her friends around her.

With only forty-eight seconds left in the game, Carbondale took the ball down the court. They passed it around for a little and then decided they were going to shoot. Paul Pippets went up for a midrange shot, but quickly passed it instead. It was an incredible pass out to LaMichael for a three. He made it. The Warriors were down two again.

The clock continued to tick down. With 28 seconds left in the game, Alex dribbled the ball down the court. The coach called time out to draw up a play.

Then a thought came into Peter's head. The article said his father hit a game winning shot. This must be the play he had heard about from his father. Peter really hoped that he didn't mess up the past now. It would be terrible if his dad missed this shot because of him.

Trenton came out of the time out and was able to pass the ball inbounds against a tough Carbondale defense. Alex set up the play. The clock was ticking down. After some movement and screens, Brady broke towards the corner. Ten seconds was left on the clock. The pass was a little off, but Brady reached out and gained control of the ball. He was falling towards the corner.

Five seconds left. Brady turns and faces the basket. He

jumps while fading away and put up the shot. The clock hit zero as the ball flew through the air right into the basket. Trenton had just won the State Championship.

Confetti was flying everywhere around the stadium. The players were hugging and celebrating with each other. The fans stormed onto the court. Taylor screamed in Peter's ear saying that she was so happy. Then she kissed him over and over. Peter did not mind this one bit.

They went out to the car, and kissed some more, then stared at the night sky together. They didn't want to start the long drive back to Trenton; they just wanted to spend time together.

Taylor left to get a drink for the road, before they headed out.

While she went inside, Peter thought about back home. He remembered his family: his mom, his dad, his apartment. He loved his family. He loved his friends back home. Even though he really only had one. Then finally, Peter looked into the night sky just as he and Taylor were doing earlier. Except this time, Peter saw a shooting star.

Great, Peter thought, *the shooting star comes right before I go cash in 100 million dollars.*

This was it. Peter had to decide whether he wanted to stay or go home. He didn't know if he would ever get another chance to go back or not.

Peter thought hard and then wished to be back in his own time. He wanted to go back. He didn't need 100 million dollars; he just wanted his real family and his real friend. Peter wanted his real home and his real time. He didn't want to mess up anything by staying in the past. Taylor was right; he belonged in the future, not the past. Tyler needed him, his family needed him. He was needed in the future. It was where he belonged.

Peter was expecting to go back almost instantly. He closed his eyes for a minute straight. Then opened them to see if that would work. Peter was still in the parking lot at the stadium in Peoria. He was sad that after making the long wish, he didn't go home. Peter apparently was stuck in 2012.

Peter wondered what he did wrong and became a bit upset. He was angry at himself for not wishing hard enough, or not wishing at the right time. Peter then realized it wasn't his fault. He just didn't know what to do anymore. He finally realized Taylor had been away for a while. He thought that she should be coming back real soon.

About five minutes later, Taylor came back with a Coke. She asked if he was ready to go and Peter said he was.

The drive home wasn't as good as it was on the way there. Peter couldn't understand why his wish didn't work this time. Eventually they got back to Trenton. When Taylor dropped Peter off, she walked him to his doorstep. They stood on his doorstep and talked.

"Peter, I had a good time tonight," Taylor said.

"I did, too," Peter agreed.

"Are you going to cash the lottery ticket?" Taylor asked.

"Yeah, I'll figure something out tomorrow."

When Taylor kissed Peter, this kiss was different than the rest. The kiss was long and tender, like she was going away for a very long time. Peter didn't understand why his wish didn't work, or why he was going to have to stay in the past.

"Will I see you tomorrow?" Peter asked.

Taylor responded, "Yeah, maybe."

Taylor wrapped her arms around Peter's waist and kissed him one last time for the night.

"Goodbye, Peter," Taylor sighed.

"Goodnight," Peter responded.

Peter thought Taylor was acting weird tonight.

And like that, Taylor left. Peter went inside, he was almost too tired from the day to stay up and think a little, but he did. He thought that tomorrow he would go to Brady and tell him about his problem. He would give him the "parent vacationing" story and hope that his family would help Peter.

Peter then thought that after he takes care of that, he could hang out with the crew.

Maybe they would want to play mini-putt again, he thought, *or maybe I can take Dad on again in another round of FIFA.* Peter eventually dozed off into a deep sleep.

CHAPTER 14

P eter woke up the next day feeling very cozy, warm covers and sheets surrounding him on his nice comfy bed. When his alarm went off, Peter didn't want to get up.

It's seven o'clock on a beautiful Sunday morning! The sun is out, the birds are chirping, and the hits are playing here on WZND radio 103.3! And here is a hit from some years back, topped out the charts for 8 straight weeks back in 2013...here is a favorite...Up to Know Good with "Mr. Moon!" the radio voice said.

Peter's eyes popped open. He didn't know where he was. He was in a big room with a plasma screen TV and a PS5 hooked up to it. There were nice clothes hanging in a huge walk-in closet. This did not look like either of his rooms.

Then the song started to play. Peter didn't understand. His father's band wasn't famous and never had a song become popular. Peter didn't know what was going on. He was in a nice room, listening to his dad's band play their number one hit about the moon.

The moon, Peter thought, *that was my idea.*

Peter then realized it actually was his idea. His dad had actually listened to him, or had he? Could this just be a dream? Peter turned the radio off, and then back on. It was true! They wrote a song about the moon and it became a huge hit. He ran out of his room and was welcomed by a huge living room. He was living in a house, a huge house.

What was going on? Peter thought.

His dad walked in through a door on Peter's left.

"Hey, bud, what's up?" Brady asked.

"Dad, what's going on? Since when do we live in this huge house?" Peter asked.

The walls were white, and there was a huge grand-piano and guitars lining the wall. The carpet was thick and warm. There was a couch with a big TV in front of it and built into the wall, there was a fish tank. It was so big, it was like an aquarium.

"What do you mean? We've lived here since you've been seven and we finished our final tour back in '27?" Brady said, a little confused. "Come on, Pete, I've told you this story thousands of times."

"Well, that song, 'Mr. Moon,' it's playing on the radio right now!" Peter said.

"Yeah, they play it a lot, it's amazing how our band was popular so long ago and we still get paychecks for radio play," Brady said to his son.

"Hey, Dad, you mind telling me some more of your childhood stories?" Peter said, very interested.

"Sure thing, buddy. Here I'll get your mom to go pick up some breakfast pizzas. And we'll talk over some breakfast."

Peter and his dad walked down the stairs leading from the

living room where they were standing. Peter was gazing at the house they were in. He wasn't for sure if this was a dream or not. If it wasn't, Peter had done the one thing he didn't want to do; affect the future while he was in the past. He continued looking at the house. The nice soft carpet continued down the stairs. Peter saw the front door and it was huge. He told his dad he would meet him in the kitchen, but that he just needed a minute.

Peter opened up the door. It was a beautiful day. He gazed around outside. The yard was so nice with its perfectly green grass and tall trees in the front. They had a long driveway leading to a road. This road looked familiar; in fact, this whole neighborhood looked familiar. Peter noticed the house across the street. It surely looked very familiar. Peter then realized that he lived in the Northland Acres! He looked at the house next to theirs. It was just as big. Peter noticed a man walking in his pajamas. The man noticed Peter.

"What's up, Pete-diggity? We are still watching football tonight, right?" the man asked.

His face looked familiar to Peter. It was a face that Peter knew well, just a little different. The man had short brown hair and some scruff on his face.

"Oh, yeah, I'll see you there," Peter said, acting like he knew what the neighbor was talking about.

Peter walked back inside. Everything was a little too weird. He found the kitchen. The floor was hardwood, and the kitchen was nice granite. There was a very nice stove and fancy refrigerator.

"Was Thomas outside? I thought I heard him yell something," Brady said while pouring two glasses of milk for Peter and himself.

Thomas? Peter thought to himself. *I just hung out with him! This is getting ridiculous!*

"Oh, yeah, he said something about watching football tonight," Peter said.

"Oh, yeah, we are going over to the Welch's to watch football with them and a bunch of our friends," Brady said.

"That's probably what he meant," Peter said.

But then, he realized that they were going over to the Welch's, as in Sarah Welch, Peter's 2035 crush.

"Oh, cool, can't wait."

"So you ready to hear some stories?" Brady said, interrupting Peter's train of thought.

Brady told his son all about his childhood. He told him stories from high school and about his friends. Peter enjoyed these stories a lot more now, considering he was a part of a lot of them.

Brady told the nugget story, the state championship story, and even about Peter. Peter was a kid who moved from Chicago and hung out with the crew for a week, but then moved back. If it wasn't for Peter, Brady never would've been with Peter's mom. Also, if it wasn't for Peter, Brady's band never would have made the song, *"Mr. Moon."* Brady said that Peter was one of the coolest kids he ever met; in fact he even told his son that was why he was named Peter.

This blew Peter's mind, *I am the reason I'm named Peter!*

After the weirdness of the whole situation, Peter thought it was all so cool. He not only changed his dad's childhood, he was a part of the stories Peter always heard before. Peter changed the outcome of his family's life.

Peter finished his pizza and then excused himself to his room. He noticed he had a cell phone on his desk. Peter had never had a cell phone before. He looked at it. He had three new text messages. Two were from Sarah Welch, which made Peter smile. They both said something about how she was looking forward to tonight. The third text was from Tyler saying that he had permission to spend the night at Peter's house after the Welch's gathering.

Peter decided that he would go outside to the backyard and further explore. He saw that they had a nice, large, fenced-in yard. Then he noticed there was a bike sitting on the porch. Peter guessed this was his bike. It wasn't like his old one. His old one was rusty and about to fall apart. This one was nice and shiny. There was also a pool and a hot tub. Peter thought this was insane. If it wasn't 65 degrees outside, Peter would have jumped right into the pool.

Peter pretty much spent the rest of the day looking around the house and finding new things. He played some FIFA 35 on the PS5.

Then his dad told him to get dressed for the Welch's. Peter searched his closet. It was full of really nice clothes. They were all name-brands and many of them still had the tags on them. Peter put on some jeans and a collared shirt and walked with his family across the street to the Welch's.

When they rang the doorbell, a man opened it. By his dad's greeting to the man, Peter figured out his name was Dylan. They walked into the house. It was nice, not as nice as Peter's though.

Peter walked into the party. Most of the people were adults; all of them seemed to know Peter. They all yelled stuff like, "Petey! Pete dawg!" or other old school names. Peter than noticed his dad was hanging out with a group of guys. He counted them. Counting his dad there were five of them. He noticed Thomas. This is when Thomas noticed him.

"Pete, my main man, what's up, dude?" Thomas said to Peter while shaking his hand.

"Nothing much, just enjoying the nice party," Peter said.

"Hey, Petey, you look taller since the last time I saw you," someone told Peter.

This is when Peter's father stepped in…"Alex, you say the most ridiculous things, you saw him yesterday."

"Doesn't mean he couldn't grow," Alex said.

Peter then looked at the other guys. They all looked big and successful. He looked at each face and could see the same person he saw back in 2012. He figured out the tall blonde haired man was Mitch. The guy with the friendly face and beard was Michael, and of course, the short one that says ridiculous things was Alex.

All of these men looked good for their age, and they all had amazing families. Michael and his wife, Zoe, had just actually had their 8th child! Zoe was showing off their newborn to all of the women at the party. Peter thought this was awesome.

Peter just hung out with the 16-year-old versions of these guys last night; in fact, he actually watched them win the state championship. Now, 23 years later, he was talking in a circle with them. This is when Peter felt a tug on his shirt. He turned around to see Sarah Welch.

"Hey, Peter!" she said smiling. "Come downstairs and hang out with us!"

She was even prettier than she ever looked before.

Peter followed her down the stairs to find a plasma screen TV, a pinball machine, and two couches. The couches were filled with Tyler and some kids from Peter's school. All the kids greeted Peter warmly and told him to sit down. Peter sat next to Sarah.

While the adults watched football upstairs, the teens decided to watch a movie. During the movie, Sarah was squeezing Peter's hand and cuddling with him. Peter definitely didn't mind this at all. About an hour into the movie, someone walked down the stairs. Sarah immediately pulled her hand away from Peter's. The lights turned on, and Sarah paused the movie.

"I brought some snacks!" Sarah's mom said, as she was walking away from the light switch.

"Thanks, Mom," Sarah chimed out in a somewhat annoyed tone.

It felt like Peter's stomach jumped right into his throat. It was Taylor. Just last night he was kissing her as she was saying goodnight. And she probably just remembers it as a childhood memory, "kissing the crazy kid who said he was from the future."

"I'll just set the snacks right here," Taylor said nicely, placing the bowl of pretzels on the coffee table.

Taylor then looked directly at Peter, gave him a wink, and went back upstairs.